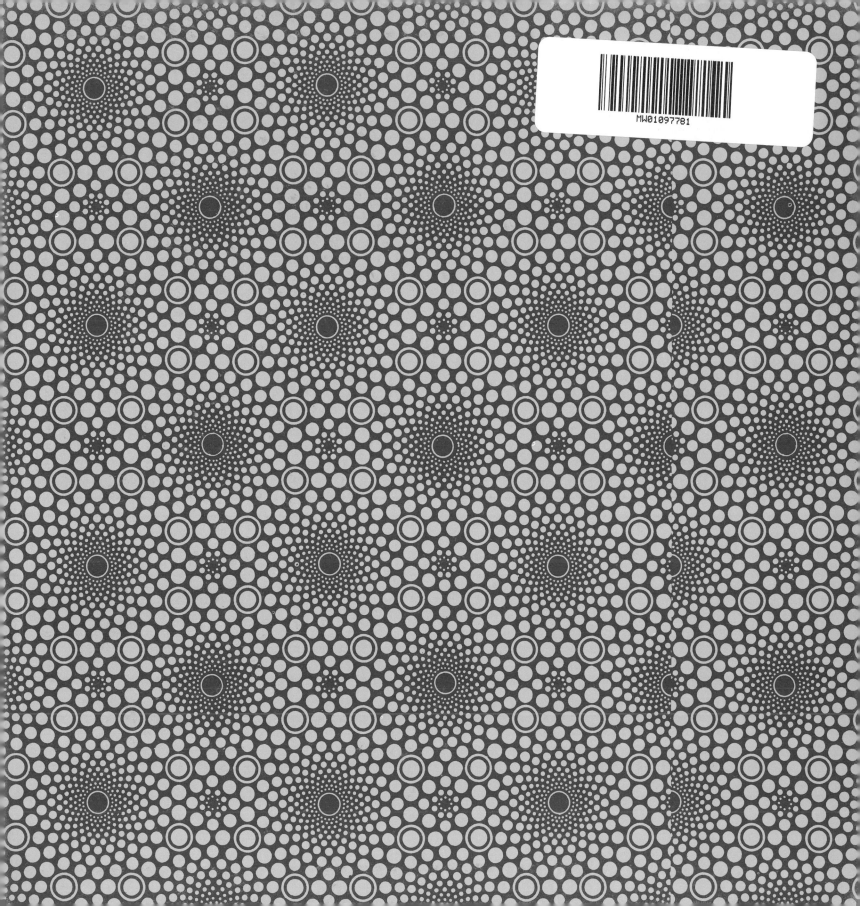

MW01097781

Miloš Macourek & Adolf Born
MAX AND SALLY
AND
THE PHENOMENAL PHONE

WELLINGTON PUBLISHING

CHICAGO

Max and Sally
and
The Phenomenal Phone

From the Czech original "Mach a Šebestová"
translated by Dagmar Herrmann

This edition first published in 1989
by
Wellington Publishing, Inc.
Chicago, Illinois

Library of Congress Cataloging-in-Publication Data

Macourek, Miloš.
  Max and Sally and the phenomenal phone.

  Translation of: Mach a Šebestová.
  Summary: As a reward for a kind deed, Max and
Sally receive a magic telephone that performs
incredible feats for its new owners.
  [l. Magic — Fiction. 2. Friendship — Fiction]
I. Born, Adolf, 1930-.....   II. Title.
PZ7.M242Max 1989   [Fic]   88-33871
ISBN 0-922984-00-X

Typeset in Baskerville by Jandon Graphics Inc, Chicago
Printed in Czechoslovakia

HOW MAX AND SALLY

GOT HOLD OF

1

THE PHENOMENAL PHONE

Max Blair and Sally Chase were third graders in Room 301.
They lived in the same apartment building and walked to school together.
Mrs. Pond and her dog Jonathan lived there too,

and so did Mrs. Shallot with Mitzi, her cat.

And when Mrs. Pond with Jonathan and Mrs. Shallot with Mitzi
ran into each other in the hall, was there a ruckus!
Mitzi sputtered like a hamster, Jonathan turned into a tiger,
Mrs. Shallot squeaked, don't worry Mitzi! Mrs. Pond yelled, quiet Jonathan!
while the other tenants peeped through the door cracks
to see what in the world was going on.
Considering this, would you blame Sally if she sometimes teased Jonathan
with her little jingle,
Hello there old Mr. Ruff,
of your noise I've had enough.
Wouldn't it drive you really bats
if there were a million cats?

That annoyed Jonathan, but otherwise he and Max and Sally were friends
and occasionally in the morning
he would run off from Mrs. Pond to walk with them to school.
Mrs. Pond did not appreciate his jaunts at all.
She would run after him shouting, Jonathan come home, Jonathan come home,
but catching Jonathan wasn't easy — Jonathan was a dog
and any dog can run faster than any Mrs. Pond.
Yet all this running wasn't completely silly,
Max and Sally got to school on time
and Mrs. Pond got some fresh air,
which is very healthy.

One day, after Max and Sally had said goodbye to Jonathan in front of the school
and sat down at their desks, Miss McGee, their teacher, walked in and said,
children, let's see now how you prepared for today's science class.
She called on Max to tell her about rabbits.
But about rabbits Max knew next to nothing.
The only rabbits he knew were Bugs Bunny and Peter
so he just kept repeating like a broken record,
the wild rabbit lives in the woods, he lives in the woods, he lives in the woods...
till the teacher stopped him and said, listen Max, even babies know
that rabbits don't live in libraries or in ice cream parlors.
Instead, why don't you tell us what rabbits feed on,
how many teeth they have — things like that!
But Max had no idea whatsoever about rabbit's teeth, so Miss McGee said,
that's enough Max, now sit down and tomorrow I'll call on you again
and you'd better shape up or else!

When school was over and everyone was going home, Max said to Sally,
lucky you, you can play now with Jonathan
while I sit at home boning up on rabbits. It's not fair!
He had hardly finished that sentence
when he noticed a strange character crawling in the grass on all fours.
Sally saw him too and said to Max,
that man's pretending to be a dog, just look at him!
But Max shook his head and said, Sally you're really nuts!
Why would an old guy like that pretend to be a dog?
I bet you he must have lost his glasses.

That was it, all right. The man had lost his glasses and was lost without them.
It's difficult to look for glasses, you know, without wearing them in the first place.
Luckily Max was wearing his and so he soon found the man's glasses
and the old gentleman was so very pleased that he told them,
listen children, since you've been so kind, look what I've got for you!
And beaming at both of them he took out of his pocket an old telephone receiver
and gave it to Sally.

Sally somewhat puzzled said, well, that's really nice of you sir,
thanks a lot sir, but could you tell us what's it for?
It's not good for calling anyone, that's for sure.
She was about to give the receiver back to the man . . .
but there was no one there to give it back to.
Now it's me who's nuts, thought Max. Where is he?
Who cares, said Sally. Better help me figure out
what to do with half a phone.
For starters, laughed Max, why don't you just say,
Hello there old Mr. Ruff?
Sally was laughing too
and said jokingly into the receiver,
Wouldn't it drive you really bats
if there were a million cats?
And after she had said it, the receiver answered,
did you say a million? Suit yourself!
Max and Sally stared, stunned,
as unbelievable scores of cats appeared around them,
tomcats and kittens, white, black, and dapple-gray,
toms sitting on the road, cats in treetops,
kittens on the rooftops,
mewing till everyone's ears buzzed.

Sally pulled herself together first and said,
Max, can you believe all these cats? The phone did this, right?
Right, said Max, but what now? What are we supposed to do with all of these cats?
I can't take them home, my parents wouldn't let me in!
Do you realize how many a million cats is?
And Sally got a bright idea, tapped her forehead and called into the receiver,
hello there, we have no idea what to do with so many cats,
so could you please take them back?

And the receiver answered, well of course, if you wish,
and then and there not a single cat was to be seen,
not a tomcat or even a kitten.

And Max said, wow, this thing really works.
That's fantastic! Do you realize what it means?
No, I don't, said Sally, but I agree with you. It's fantastic, all right.
Now let's go home.
Jonathan was sitting on the window sill, welcoming them from afar
with his barking.

Poor Jonathan, said Sally, that Mrs. Pond has locked him up again.
But Max only laughed and said, he'll be down in a jiffy, if you want him to.
And he took the receiver and asked, can Jonathan turn into a bird for a while?
Why not, the voice in the receiver said,
if you want him to be a bird, he'll be a bird.

Jonathan, now standing on the window sill, grew wings, and Max, below, shouted,
what are you waiting for, start flying!
And Jonathan flapped his wings and slowly floated down,
landing right in front of Sally.
Poor Jonathan looked quite peculiar. The wings didn't suit him at all.
Max turned up his nose. Listen Sally, he said,
we can't play with such an awful-looking creature, really!

But Sally said, don't let it worry you Max, you've got to study.
Remember the rabbits? You'll be called on tomorrow.
Max just laughed. I've got a great idea!
Rabbits, you said? Why couldn't the three of us play with rabbits right now?
And he said into the receiver,
we've got this terrible urge to become rabbits, could we please?
I don't see why not, answered the receiver,
you want to be rabbits — go right ahead and be rabbits.
And no sooner said than done, Max, Sally and Jonathan
became rabbits and they hopped into the woods.

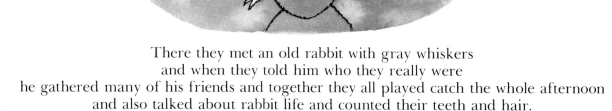

There they met an old rabbit with gray whiskers
and when they told him who they really were
he gathered many of his friends and together they all played catch the whole afternoon
and also talked about rabbit life and counted their teeth and hair.
So the next day when the teacher called on Max
he told her not only how many top teeth and how many bottom teeth rabbits have
but also how many hairs they have on their bellies and how many on their backs
and then spoke for almost an hour about how many children they have
and how the baby rabbits play and what they like to eat for lunch and what for dinner
and what time they go to sleep and when they get up again.
Miss McGee couldn't believe her ears and said to herself,
could it be that a third grader would know more about rabbits than I do?
And she gave Max a giant A+ and Max sat down smiling and Sally whispered to him,
wow, that phone is really phenomenal!
And Max nodded, you said it, and you ain't seen nothin' yet!
We'll have fun with it, that's for sure!

HOW MAX AND SALLY

CONVINCED MRS. POND THAT

2

SHE HAD THE BEST DOG IN THE WORLD

One day as Max and Sally were leaving for school, Jonathan saw them
and zip! he ran away from Mrs. Pond and followed his friends.
He noticed that Max and Sally
had lunchboxes but no books,
and he kept shaking his head, thinking,
this doesn't make any sense, why only lunchboxes?
till Sally told him, listen Jonathan, today we don't need books
because there's no school today.
We're going on a field trip to Moose Lake. Do you understand what I'm saying?

Jonathan began to whine, why why why,
and Max said, listen Sally, that dog's whining for real.
I've got a feeling he'd like to join us. Know what I mean?
But Sally said, Miss McGee wouldn't let a dog come with us
and come to think of it, Mrs. Pond wouldn't like it either.
Just look, there she is, running after Jonathan already.
And in fact Mrs. Pond was running as fast she could, yelling,
Jonathan come home this very minute!

But that very minute Max got an idea and said to Sally,
now tell me why do we have
that phenomenal phone if we don't use it?
We'll change Jonathan into a boy and that will do it.
And right away he said into the receiver,
please, we need to have Jonathan
looking like a boy carrying a lunchbox.
So when Mrs. Pond finally arrived,
what did she see?
Max and Sally
and a boy with big ears sticking out carrying a lunchbox,
and she wondered why Jonathan wasn't around, saying,
I'll be... I thought he was with you!
But Sally only shrugged her shoulders and said,
he was here just a minute ago, Mrs. Pond.
And that was nothing but the truth
so Sally wasn't really lying at all.

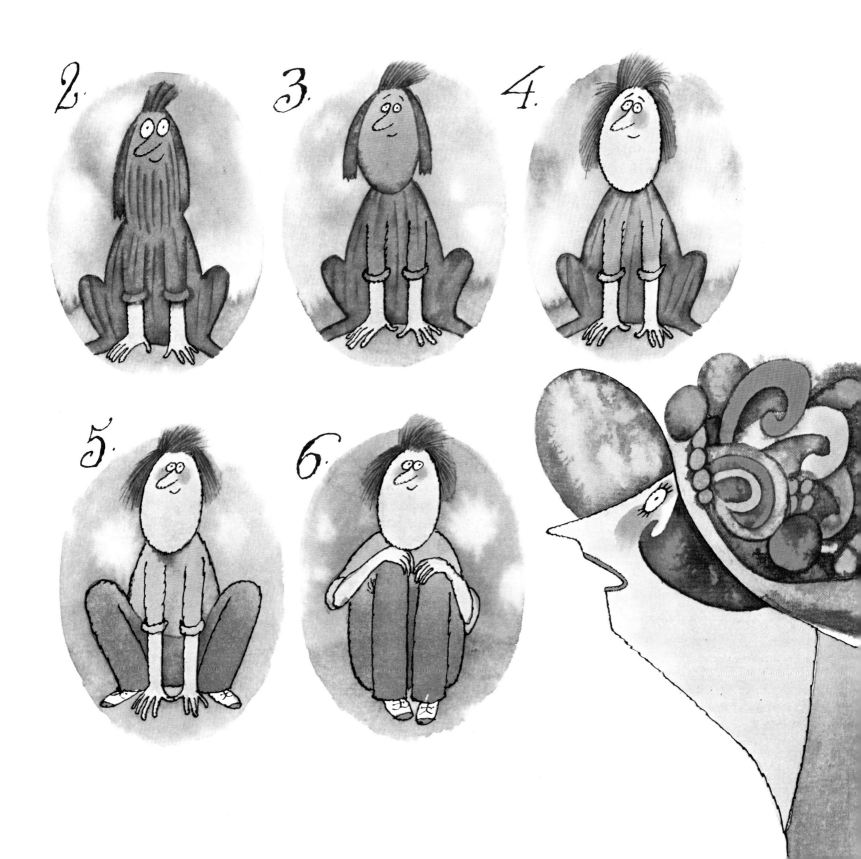

Mrs. Pond went home grumbling to herself,
just you wait Jonathan, you'll get it when you come back!
But Jonathan went wild with joy
at being rid of Mrs. Pond for a while.
He was just so happy
he kept running and jumping around Max and Sally.
Sally only shook her head, I don't know, I don't know,
somehow this doesn't look right to me.
That dog looks like a perfectly normal kid with a lunchbox,
but he's still acting like a dog.
Max scratched his head and sighed,
you're right, Sally, you're right,
I've got the same feeling. This won't turn out.
And sure enough, when they reached the bus
and Sally asked the teacher
if their friend Jonathan Terrier could come with them,
Jonathan spoiled everything.
He whined and jumped up,
gave the teacher a big lick on her cheek
and on her nose, and he even started to bark.
And Miss McGee thought, what a bizarre child!
A real troublemaker, this one, and they want me to take him with us on a trip!
Well, that's really all I need.
He'll make a fuss and keep behaving like a dog,
as if it were not enough already
that Ralph's coming along, that naughty boy.
So she said,
I'm sorry but there really isn't a seat left on the bus,
so let's go, children, let's go now.
And they left.

But wasn't Jonathan Max's and Sally's friend?
And to be someone's friend, that's no small potatoes.
Would a friend leave his friends just like that? Jonathan certainly wouldn't.
So he ran along after the bus, dust flying behind him, right down the highway,
zooming around the curves, and through the back window
the kids waved at him and held their thumbs up.

When the bus finally stopped at Moose Lake,
not only Max and Sally but all the third graders cheered
because Jonathan had made it,
he had run that long way just to spend the day with his friends.
And Miss McGee said to herself,
this Jonathan is really a strange kid and his manners leave a lot to be desired
but there definitely is something good in him —
in fact there is something good in everybody.
Then it dawned on her that in those lunchboxes there was something good too,
so she clapped her hands and said,
now children, why don't you get your lunch
and eat the treats your mothers have packed for you.
And all the kids dove into their desserts,
all kinds of pies and cakes and apple turnovers,
only poor Sally couldn't find a thing in her lunchbox
even though her mom had baked a real treat for her
and had packed a large slice of strawberry pie.
Sally was so unhappy that she said to Miss McGee,
someone must have taken a slice of strawberry pie out of my lunchbox
and didn't leave even a tiny bit for me, not even a crumb!
And the teacher said, who would do something like that?
Raise your hand whoever did it! But nobody raised a hand
and all of them said, what's going to happen now?
There's a thief here and we don't know who it is.
But for Jonathan this was no big deal,
on the contrary it was a trifle
since it just so happened he was an expert in these matters.
Well, you know, a dog is a dog.
He sniffed here and snuffed there
and in no time was carrying a lunchbox to Miss McGee.

When Miss McGee opened the lunchbox,
there was a slice of strawberry pie staring right at her,
and the lunchbox had Ralph's name on it.
Well, wouldn't you know it, it's Ralph's.
That boy again!
Shame on you, Ralph! I don't even want to look at you!
She wanted to thank Jonathan in front of all the children
but Jonathan was busy just then
for he had spotted a cat in a tree and zoom! off he went.
You know, a dog is a dog, and when a dog spots a cat there's no stopping him.
And the teacher said to herself,
Well, I'll be! He's such a bright boy — detects a thief in no time —
but a moment later behaves like a fool.
She kept shaking her head, quite puzzled.

Now Ralph wasn't the least embarrassed,
and instead of being ashamed of what he had done
he was showing off, pretending to be a champion diver,
standing on the edge of the lake bragging,
just watch this jump,
you haven't seen anything like it before, one-two-three!

And as soon as he had jumped in, he began bobbing up and down,
sputtering and screaming he-e-lp, he-e-lp!
It was awful. The kids were screaming,
Ralph is drowning, please help, please, he's drowning!
The teacher was clutching her head,
that's all I need, oh, that Ralph again,
goodness, what will the parents say!
But Jonathan just hopped into the water
and pulled Ralph out right away.

And Miss McGee sighed with relief
and made the class stand together as if for a picture and asked Jonathan
not to run off chasing cats again,
and then she said, we ought to express our gratitude to Jonathan Terrier
for his heroic act of bravery and courage.
But Jonathan wasn't used to such pomp and didn't know what to do with himself
so he began to scratch with his foot behind his ears as if he had fleas
and kept scratching himself
faster and faster all the time.

The teacher was aghast.
She stiffened and gasped, that's more than I can possibly tolerate!
Such an intelligent boy and devoted friend
behaving in this absolutely horrid manner!
But Max said, excuse me, we've got to tell you,
er, well, actually, how should I put it?
Jonathan isn't a boy at all, really, he is a dog.
And Sally said, it's our friend Jonathan the dog
and because we like him a lot we wanted to take him with us on the trip.
And Max said something into the phenomenal phone
and, no sooner said than done, Jonathan turned into a dog again.
All the kids just stared flabbergasted
but Miss McGee immediately offered Jonathan a ham and cheese sandwich
and said, forgive me Jonathan if I judged you too harshly.
And on the way back Jonathan travelled in comfort like a prince,
and the whole class walked him home,
and when Mrs. Pond began scolding him for being all wet
and saying that a well-bred dog ought to lie on the sofa at home
and not run around all day long,
Miss McGee asked her if she wasn't by any chance mistaking the dog for a pillow.
A pillow can lie on a sofa forever and it won't mind it a bit, she said,
but a dog is a dog
and your Jonathan is without a doubt the best dog in the whole world
as I discovered right off!
Well, Mrs. Pond felt a little ashamed and said,
all right, I won't lock Jonathan up any more
and whenever he wants to play with Max and Sally I'll always let him.
And Jonathan began barking happily, ruff ruff ruff,
and Max and Sally started singing along and all the children clapped their hands
and even Mrs. Pond and Miss McGee cheered
and whoever happened to be passing by had to say,
by golly, I haven't heard that much joy in a long time.

HOW MAX AND SALLY
CURED CHARLIE BEAN'S

3

STREP THROAT

One day, just before school was over, Miss McGee told the children,
tomorrow we'll go to the zoo, just as I've promised.
You can imagine how very pleased the kids were,
they were looking forward to seeing the kangaroos and the monkeys.
Sally said, that's great! But how about Charlie?
He's got strep throat. Does that mean he won't be coming with us?
The teacher just shrugged her shoulders and said, well, Sally,
a strep throat is a nasty thing,
the human body needs about a week to conquer the treacherous germs.
Charlie will have to stay at home and we can't do anything about that.
I'm sorry, we'll have to go to the zoo without him.

On their way home from school, passing by Charlie's house,
they saw poor Charlie's sad face staring at them from behind the window,
and Max and Sally felt awfully sorry for him so Sally said,
it may be true that the human body needs a week
to conquer the treacherous germs,
but I bet we finish them off in five minutes.
And Max said sure, why else do we have the phenomenal phone?

And right after lunch they armed themselves to the teeth.
Max had a rope, a small hammer, and a huge fork from the carving set,
Sally had a bucket and a brush,
and that's how they headed for Charlie's house, with Jonathan of course.
When they arrived Charlie was asleep and Mrs. Bean told them,
just be quiet please, I am so glad that Charlie's finally fallen asleep,
you know sleep makes one stronger. I wouldn't want you to wake him up.
And Max said, us? waking him up? no way!
But could we please just wait here till he wakes?
Don't worry about us, we'll be just fine.

And hardly had Mrs. Bean closed the door behind her
when Max said to the receiver,
we'd like to become tiny enough to fight our friend Charlie Bean's germs,
and the receiver answered, just watch out, germs are awfully tricky! Good luck to you!
And Max, Sally and Jonathan instantly became smaller than a toothbrush,
then smaller than a thimble, and they kept getting smaller
till a breadcrumb seemed to them bigger than a four story house
and that was just small enough
to launch an attack upon Charlie's germs.

Let's go! they shouted and jumped into Charlie's mouth.
As they were creeping inside they saw Charlie's huge tongue.
It wasn't red and clear like tongues should be
but full of spots, and Max said to Sally,
can you see what those wretched germs have done? They'll pay for this!
Sally was trying to scrape those spots but stopped
when Jonathan barked at them a warning.
Max and Sally looked around and got terribly frightened
for above them they saw about six hundred eighty germs
gnawing on Charlie's tonsils like they were the tastiest thing in the world,
smacking their lips horribly.
It was gruesome.

Sally couldn't stand it and screamed,
stop it! and the germs did, really,
but then they began to growl
and charged full tilt against Max and Sally.

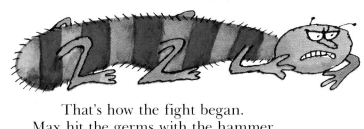

That's how the fight began.
Max hit the germs with the hammer
and stabbed them with the fork,
Sally brandished the bucket and pounded with it right and left,
and Jonathan, showing his teeth, attacked the beastly creatures
till their fur flew.

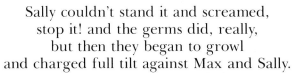

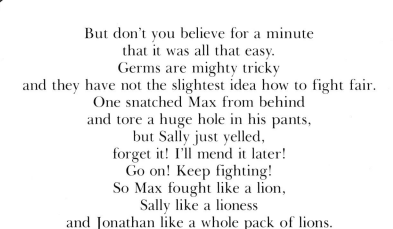

But don't you believe for a minute
that it was all that easy.
Germs are mighty tricky
and they have not the slightest idea how to fight fair.
One snatched Max from behind
and tore a huge hole in his pants,
but Sally just yelled,
forget it! I'll mend it later!
Go on! Keep fighting!
So Max fought like a lion,
Sally like a lioness
and Jonathan like a whole pack of lions.

Just then, Charlie awoke feeling like something was going on in his throat and called,
mommy, mommy, my throat, ow, it's worse than yesterday,
and Mrs. Bean clasped her hands and right away called
Doctor Sorley who said,
well well, that doesn't sound good to me, that doesn't sound good at all,
I'm already on my way,
but in the meantime, why don't you make Charlie some warm tea with lemon.

The good doctor shouldn't have suggested the tea.
Like a flood, the warm stream of tea
soaked Max, Sally and Jonathan dreadfully
and almost washed them away.
They held onto Charlie's tonsils
which wasn't exactly easy
since the tonsils, as you well know, have no handles to grab.
In short, they were holding on, but just barely,
when Mrs. Bean said, Charlie, come on,
drink it down, this sipping does no good.
So Charlie took a real gulp
and Max, Sally and Jonathan were suddenly gone from his throat.
They flew down like they were on a waterslide,
tumbling faster and faster,
Sally squeaking,
Jonathan whining,
and Max saying to himself,
gosh, if Charlie only knew what he has done to us with this tea.
When is this trip going to end?

And then, splash, they dove, and found themselves swimming in a lake
on the bottom of an enormous cave.
Something like an iceberg was sticking out of it
and Sally said, where are we, Max?
Are these icebergs or what?
And Max said, would you please stop being silly?
Can't you see? It's toast with butter!
Charlie must have had it for breakfast. Climb on!
So all three of them climbed on that piece of toast
and Max said, this enormous cave we are in, that's Charlie's stomach.
You wouldn't have guessed, would you? And the lake, that's tea with lemon,
and he was about to go on explaining
when Sally grabbed his hand and screamed,
look, Max, do you see what's floating in that tea?
And Max looked and saw thousands of germs floating all around,
well, actually about six hundred eighty of them
and all of them dead as dead can be,
which figured, because if you hit a germ with a hammer,
it's finished all right, and if you drown it, it's had it for good.
And Sally said, well they're finished, but so are we.
We won't get out of here in one piece, I'm telling you.
But Max said, c'mon Sally, keep your chin up!
A man of courage will always manage, just watch!
And Max began blowing into the hot tea,
and the toast they were standing on began floating toward the wall of the cave.
Max then tied the rope which they had brought with them to Jonathan's collar
and Jonathan nipped into the wall once
and then again a little higher
and then again a little higher
and Max and Sally held onto the rope, climbing behind him.
And as they were climbing, Max said,
Sally, where's that bucket and the brush? We may yet need it!
And Sally said, when it comes to cleaning,
you'd better leave things to me.

When Doctor Sorley arrived at Charlie's house and Charlie stuck out his tongue and said aaahhh,
Doctor Sorley gave it one look and cried, I can't believe it!
This is absolutely astounding, Mrs. Bean!
I certainly wouldn't say that Charlie's throat is worse than yesterday,
on the contrary, Charlie's throat is absolutely perfect!
Why don't you have a look yourself. No sign of germs at all!
Even the tongue looks much better.

And he was right, because Sally had just given it a nice brushing
till it was red and clean.
And Max cried, we did it! and he pulled out the receiver and helloed,
mission accomplished! Get us out of here, please!
Mrs. Bean's mouth dropped open, Charlie gazed,
Doctor Sorley's eyes bulged and all three stared first at each other,

and then at Sally, at Jonathan and at Max,
with his torn pants, standing at Charlie's bedside.
And Sally was saying, now Charlie, what are you doing here as if you were sick?
Cheer up, your strep's gone and all over with! Now hop out of that bed!
And the good doctor nodded, that's right my dear lady,
those children are absolutely right, your son is as fit as a fiddle.
And Charlie scooted out of his bed yelling,
so tomorrow I can go to the zoo, I can go to the zoo
to see the monkeys and the kangaroo,
tra-la-la-la, tra-la-la.
He danced around like mad
and Max, and Sally, and Jonathan did too,
all three of them so very happy
about a job well done.

HOW MAX AND SALLY
LIVED THROUGH A HAIRY DAY

4

AT THE ZOO

The day Room 301 went to the zoo Miss McGee was in such a good mood,
she let Jonathan come with Max and Sally.
The day started splendidly and everything went smoothly,
as the children walked nicely along, thoughtfully peering
at the kangaroos and the monkeys, the polar bears and the lions,

at the funny penguins that always look as if they're dressed in tuxedos.

They looked at the elephants and then at the hippos for a while,

and all the children behaved. They behaved remarkably well, actually,
except for Ralph and Jerry, as usual.
Although the signs DON'T FEED THE ANIMALS were everywhere,
those two couldn't have cared less.
They kept throwing peanut butter sandwiches, apples and cookies,
in fact, their whole lunch, into the monkey cages.

Soon after, a tremendous commotion broke out
around the monkeys. People in white
coats began running back and forth.
Do you want to know why? I'll tell you.
Their most famous monkey had suddenly
turned green, green like a freshly
painted bench in the park. That's why.
And the chief curator was screaming,
Of course it's green!
Why is it green?
It's sick to its stomach,
that's why!
It may die...
oh my, oh my,
such a rare specimen,
the only one
on the whole continent!

1.

The chief curator and his assistant
immediately began to pump out the poor monkey's stomach
and it looked as if that monkey was going to faint any moment.
All one could see was the white of its eyes.
It was awful.

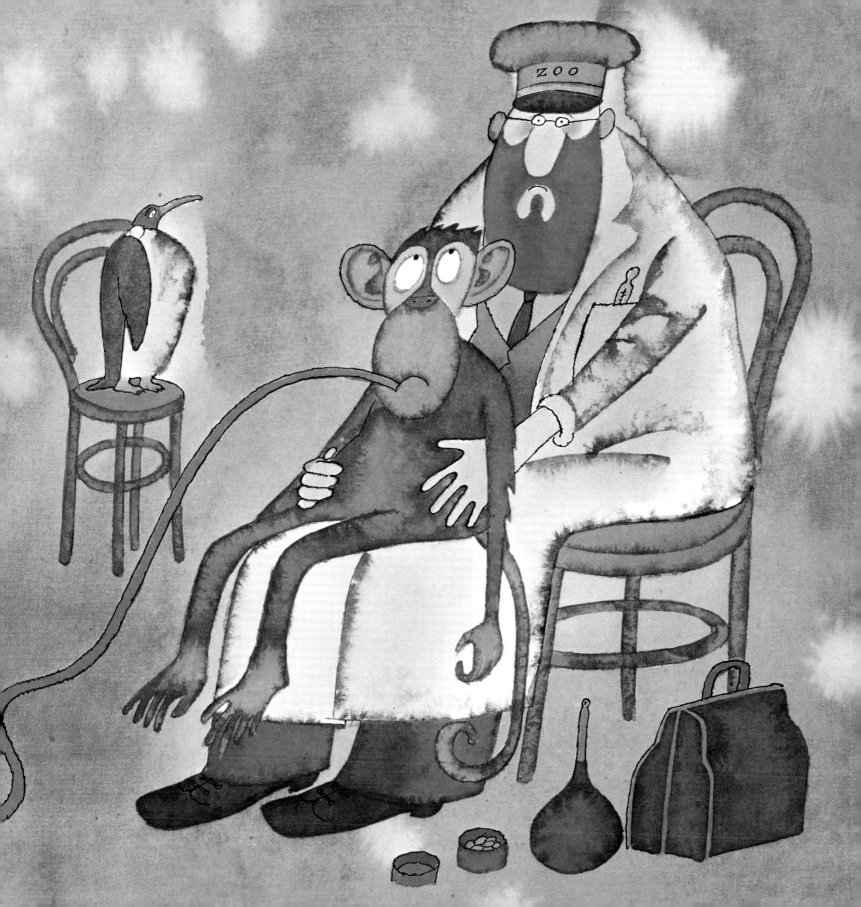

And Miss McGee became terribly upset with Ralph and with Jerry too,
and said, how can you be so mean? Why would anyone make those poor animals suffer?
They've never done you any harm, have they? Don't you pity them even just a little?

Or did you do it because they can't tell on you, because they can't defend themselves?
If they could only talk I'm sure they'd speak their minds.
Then you'd hear something!

Max blinked at Sally. Animals speaking? he said, that could be interesting.
So Sally pulled out the receiver and whispered into it,
we'd like those animals to speak,
and the voice from the receiver said, very well, as you wish,
if you want those animals to talk they will talk.

Can you imagine the shock when all of a sudden the giraffe said,
Ralph, Ralph, you're really a little monster and you Jerry are just the same.
I would have never believed it just from looking at you.
Jonathan shook his head in agreement and said,

dear Miss Giraffe, that Ralph boy, you don't have to tell me about him.
I know him better than I'd care to.
On the trip to Moose Lake
he stole a slice of strawberry pie from Sally here,
so what would you expect from such a bad boy,
tell me that.
And the elephant flapped his ears and spoke in his bass voice,
let me tell you something, I am just a simple elephant,
I never went to school,
but I'd surely never do anything so nasty
as to make someone sick on purpose.
Now Miss McGee had stiffened. She had become still as a statue,
just gazing, her mouth wide open.

The whole third grade stared in disbelief while everyone else just marveled.
The director of the zoo came running with his assistant right behind him
who couldn't believe his eyes and cried, how come those animals can speak?
I am going to write a book about this starting right now!
He pulled out his fountain pen and began scribbling. Today, he wrote,
three animals, all mammals, a giraffe, a dog and an elephant started talking
just like people do…but as he quickly wrote

a tortoise said, sir you wouldn't mind adding me to that list,
would you?
I also speak,

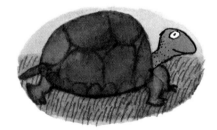

and a penguin said, of course,
we all speak, don't we.

And the teacher, clasping her hands, wailed, what will happen in school now?
A fine mess, that's all I need, mammals bawling people out, birds complaining,
science going topsy turvy, I'll have to throw away all my old tests,
what a horror, how will we manage?

Max whispered, listen Sally, isn't this getting to be a bit too much?
Shouldn't we put a stop to it? Say, who knows what all this will do
to my A+ in science.
And Sally nodded and was about to reach for the receiver
when she realized she didn't have it.
A giraffe had pulled it from Sally's pocket
and now it was sticking out of the giraffe's mouth.
Sally pulled Max by his sleeve. Max, look at that giraffe...
Before she could finish the sentence
the giraffe opened its mouth, the receiver fell into the crocodile's open muzzle,
the crocodile gobbled it up
and before anyone could utter a word
the receiver was gone.

What are we going to do now? That's what I'd like to know, said Sally.
We can't simply leave that receiver in the crocodile's belly.
No kidding, said Max. Well let's think of something and fast.
Just then, Max noticed Jonathan and right away he got an idea.
Sally, I've got it! Jonathan will help. He took Jonathan aside and said to him,
listen Jonathan, now that I can talk to you like man to man
what would you say if I asked you to slip into that crocodile's belly
for just a second and fish out our phenomenal phone?
And Jonathan answered without missing a beat, are you kidding me?
Do you think I'd let myself be eaten by a beast like that? What do you think I am?
A nitwit? Do me a favor, pal, count me out. Well, so long, got to go.
But Max caught up with him and said,
Jonathan wait, would you listen to me please?
If that little old croc gave you his word of honor
that he wouldn't eat you up, then nothing would happen to you, silly.
And Jonathan said to himself, well, I suppose that makes sense,
and so he talked it over with the crocodile who was really an old and wise croc
and who promised not to harm him.
So Jonathan entered the croc's enormous muzzle.
But what happened then was shocking and totally unexpected.
The crocodile clicked his upper and lower teeth together and swallowed Jonathan
like a raspberry.

Congratulations, said Sally.
Now we've lost the receiver, and Jonathan to boot.
If that's what you wanted, you've got it!
Have you lost all your marbles?
Never heard about the crocodile being a sly and blood-thirsty animal?

At that the crocodile said in a loud voice,
excuse me, Miss Chase, you are wrong as wrong can be,
I am not sly nor am I blood-thirsty.
All I want is to prevent more trouble, nothing else.
And that's why I won't let Jonathan out
unless Ralph and Jerry and all of you third graders
give me your word of honor
that you will never again feed the animals in the zoo, and I mean NEVER!
And Miss McGee said, well how about that, children,
you've heard the reptile's wise words.
Do you have anything to say?
And the director of the zoo and his assistant,
the chief curator and his assistant, the visitors,
and also the penguins, the kangaroos, the polar bears, the giraffes, monkeys,
lions, tortoises, elephants and hippos,
all repeated after the teacher,

well, children, do you have anything to say?
And the kids felt really sorry for Jonathan
and also for the green monkey,
so they gave the crocodile their word of honor,
even Ralph and Jerry did, honest.
The old crocodile then opened his enormous jaws
and out walked Jonathan with the receiver.
And Miss McGee, the zoo director and his assistant,
the chief curator and his assistant,
all the animals, everybody cheered,
and Room 301 went home happy.
Max and Sally were so-o-o-o relieved,
and looked forward to many more adventures
with their phenomenal phone.